Aa Bb Cc Dd

Ee Ff Gg Hh Ii

Jj Kk Ll Mm Nn

Oo Pp Qq Rr Ss

Tt Uu Vv Ww

Xx Yy Zz

alphabet rescue

by **AUDREY WOOD**
illustrated by **BRUCE WOOD**

THE BLUE SKY PRESS
An Imprint of Scholastic Inc. • New York

THE BLUE SKY PRESS

Text copyright © 2006 by Audrey Wood

Illustrations copyright © 2006 by Bruce Wood

Library of Congress catalog card number: 2005032382

ISBN 0-439-85316-8

10 9 8 7 6 5 4 3 2 1   06 07 08 09 10

Printed in Singapore   46

First printing, September 2006

The illustrations in this book were created digitally using various

3-D modeling software packages, assisted by Adobe Photoshop.

Designed by Bruce Wood and Kathleen Westray

To Eva Mahina Chupity—A.W.

To Olaf Negard—B.W.

The little letters in Charley's Alphabet had worked hard all year long in school, helping him learn to read and write. As Charley packed to visit his grandparents, his alphabet took off on a pencil.

They were ready for a vacation, too.
The little letters soared past the moon to Alphabet City,
the place where they were made.

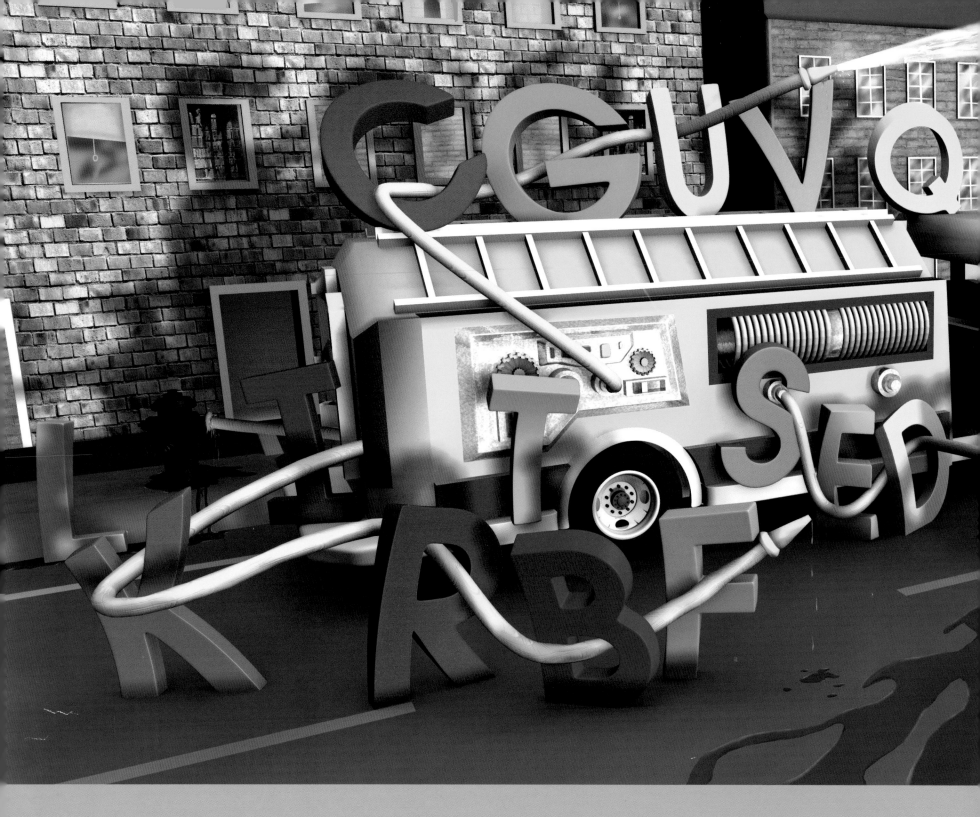

The next morning, Charley's Alphabet came across some capital letters with a new fire engine. They were practicing with their big fire hoses.

"Let us try, please!" the little letters begged.
"Well, OK," Fire Chief **F** said. "Just for a minute."

But when the little letters tried, the hose whipped around
like a wild snake, spraying all of the capital letters.

"Fire hoses are for big letters only!" Fire Chief **F** exclaimed.
"Go and play where you won't get into trouble!"

Behind the firehouse they discovered an old, broken-down fire engine.
Little **e** and Little **x** had an excellent idea. "Let's rescue it!" they exclaimed.

All the little letters searched until they found what
was needed to fix up the old fire truck.

When they were finished, it looked fantastic.

"Clang! Clang!" Little **b** rang the fire-engine bell as they drove away.
Soon they came to some letters trying to wash a very dirty car.

"To the rescue!" Little **r** shouted as they turned on their fire hoses.

Before long, they were aiming them perfectly, and the car was sparkling clean.

Further down the road, they heard sad cries for help. Three letters had climbed too high in a tree, and they were afraid to come down.

"Our fire engine has ladders and nets!" Little **n** shouted.
"We will rescue you!"

As the sun set beyond the city, Charley's little letters noticed an angry cloud of smoke in the sky.

"Look!" Little **f** exclaimed. "The letter-making factory is on fire!"

"If the factory burns," Little **x** said, "that would be extra bad. Children won't have alphabets to learn at school!"

"Whhooooo-wheeeeeeeee!" A loud siren sounded.
The capital letters were speeding down the road on
their big fire engine toward the factory.

But as they passed by, a tire blew out. The big truck spun out of control and rolled over! None of the capitals were hurt, but they were scattered everywhere!

When the little letters saw that the big fire engine was broken,
they came to the rescue again.

"Climb aboard, capitals!" Little c called. "Our fire engine can fight the fire!"

All of the letters hung on tightly as the little engine sped to the fire.

At the factory, the letters aimed their hoses

and sprayed water into the boiling smoke and fire.

Inside the factory, they used their ladders and nets to rescue

a new batch of Little e's trapped on a burning balcony.

At last the fire was out.

"Clang! Clang!" Fire Chief **F** rang the fire-engine bell.

Then he announced, "Charley's little letters and their fantastic fire engine are welcome at our firehouse any time!"

The next day, as they rode in a parade through the streets of Alphabet City, the alphabet heroes were cheered by everyone.

At the end of the parade, some of the new letters that had been saved from ruin spelled out a message to Charley's Alphabet . . . thank you—thank you—thank you.

The little letters returned home just in time. Charley's vacation had ended, too. He needed his little letters to help him write an important card to his grandparents.

So they did.

Aa Bb Cc Dd

Ee Ff Gg Hh Ii

Jj Kk Ll Mm Nn

Oo Pp Qq Rr Ss

Tt Uu Vv Ww

Xx Yy Zz